Tell the TRUTH

First published in the UK in 2008 by
QED Publishing
A Quarto Group company
226 City Road
London EC1V 2TT
www.qed-publishing.co.uk

A catalogue record for this book is available from the British Library.

ISBN 978 1 84835 076 2

Author Kate Tym
Illustrator Sarah Wade
Editor Clare Weaver
Designer Alix Wood
Consultant David Hart

Publisher Steve Evans
Creative Director Zeta Davies

Printed and bound in China

Tania Mortimer's mummy was very good at baking cakes.

When Tania Mortimer's baby sister was one,
her mummy made
the Best Cake EVER
for her birthday tea.

TEA COFFEE

4

Mummy left it on the kitchen table and went
to wake Baby Brenda from her sleep.

Tania was left alone
in the kitchen with
the Best Cake
EVER.

Tania looked at it. It looked at her.

It seemed to be saying
"Go on Tania,
have a little bit...
Mummy won't notice
one little bit."

Well... thought Tania.

Yes... thought Tania.

Perhaps one little bit...
thought Tania.

Tania looked at the pile of
crumbs that used to be
the Best Cake EVER.

She felt very bad.
Mummy was going to be
really mad.

"It wasn't me," said Tania.

"Cake burglars crept in and tried to steal Baby Brenda's cake, and I tried to stop them."

"In fact," said Tania, "they weren't human burglars. They were **alien** burglars and they **transformogrifacted** themselves into the kitchen.

They had to take the cake, they need sweets to keep their planet **alive**..."

"In fact," said Tania, "they sucked the cake up into their spaceship using their cake sucker-a-matic machine."

12

"And I got covered in cake because I jumped on the cake to try and STOP them taking it," said Tania.

"I was really rather brave."

"You were!" said Mummy. "You were very brave. But this is terrible. We can't have alien burglars coming and stealing our cakes. I must call the police, and the paper and Daddy!"

Tania felt terrible. She also felt a bit sick, partly because she'd eaten so much cake and partly because she knew she'd done something really bad.

She'd eaten all the cake and then she'd lied about it.

NOW Mummy thought she was a hero and was going to call the police!

"Hello," said Mummy, "is that the Editor-in-Chief? Alien burglars came into my kitchen and stole **the Best Cake EVER.** My daughter fought them off – you must put it on the front page!"

Tania's knees started to **Wobble**

"Hello," said Mummy, "is that Daddy?

Alien burglars came into the kitchen and stole the Best Cake EVER. You must come home immediately!"

Tania couldn't take any more.

"IT WAS ME!" she shouted. "I ate the cake. There were NO alien burglars, there was NO transformogrifacation, there was NO spaceship and NO cake-sucker-a-matic machine.

And I didn't have to stop them. I got covered in cake because... because... *because...*"

"I ate the cake," said Tania. "And I'm sorry!"

Mummy looked relieved.

"Thank goodness for that," she said. "I'm glad there aren't any alien cake burglars in our neighbourhood and I'm really, really glad you told the truth. That was brave of you."

And after Mummy had phoned the police, the paper and Daddy again, Tania and Baby Brenda and Mummy all baked a brand new cake.

When they had finished,
they all had to agree –
this cake really was

the Best Cake EVER

– and that's no lie!

TEA

COFFEE

SUGAR

Notes for Parents and Teachers

- Look at the front cover of the book together. Talk about the picture. Can the children guess what the book is going to be about? Read the title together.

- Read page 6. Discuss with the children what emotion Tania is feeling when she thinks the cake is talking to her.

- When Tania looks at the pile of crumbs, why does she feel bad (page 8)? Why does she think Mummy is going to be mad? Talk about trust with the children. Mummy trusted Tania to be left alone in the kitchen with the cake. Part of trust is doing the right thing when you are left alone.

- Read page 10 together. Why does Tania say it wasn't her when it was? Point out that although Tania is worried about getting into trouble for eating the cake, shouldn't she also be worried about getting into trouble for lying? Discuss with the children which is worse, doing something wrong, or lying about it.

- Look at pages 11–13. Talk about the nature of lying with the children – how one lie tends to lead to another and how the hole you dig for yourself can get bigger and bigger.

- On page 15 Tania has portrayed herself as a hero. Now she feels terrible. Why do the children think she feels like this?

- Discuss pages 16–17 with the children. Mummy calls the police and the newspaper. Tania's knees start to wobble. Why is this? What will happen if the police and the newspaper people do come to the house? Talk about Tania having to continue the lie and how things could escalate.

- On page 19, why can't Tania take it any more? How is trying to keep up the lie making her feel? Do the children think she feels relieved once she's told Mummy? Why isn't Mummy cross? What does Mummy mean when she says it was brave of Tania to tell the truth?

- Read page 20 together. Discuss the fact that mummies and daddies often know when children are telling fibs, which is why it's better not to.

- Tania's mummy and Baby Brenda all have fun baking a new cake together (page 21). Does Tania's mummy still love Tania even though she did something wrong? Explain to the children that parents always love their children no matter what they've done. Sometimes their mummy or daddy may not like what they've done, but they still like them.

- Do the children think Tania has learned her lesson? Do they think she would lie about something she's done in future?

- Relate the story of the Little Boy who Cried Wolf to the children. What happens if you tell lies all the time?